Raven's HeartSong

Written and Illustrated

Teresa Marie Tipton, PhD

AuthorHouse™ UK
1663 Liberty Drive
Bloomington, IN 47403 USA
www.authorhouse.co.uk
UK TFN: 0800 0148641 (Toll Free inside the UK)
UK Local: 02036 956322 (+44 20 3695 6322 from outside the UK)

Because of the dynamic nature of the Internet, any web addresses or links contained in this book may have changed since publication and may no longer be valid. The views expressed in this work are solely those of the author and do not necessarily reflect the views of the publisher, and the publisher hereby disclaims any responsibility for them.

Any people depicted in stock imagery provided by Getty Images are models, and such images are being used for illustrative purposes only.
Certain stock imagery © Getty Images.

This book is printed on acid-free paper.

ISBN: 978-1-6655-9631-2 (sc)
ISBN: 978-1-6655-9632-9 (e)

Print information available on the last page.

Published by AuthorHouse 06/24/2022

author HOUSE®

Acknowledgements

This book is dedicated with gratitude to my parents Betty Jane and Charles Muzzy Tipton, for their exampled love of reading and encouragement to write books. My mother inspired my writing with a birthday present of the Diaries of Anais Nin when I was 16. My father instilled the love of a good story from his impromptu bedtime stories and the perseverance to never give up finishing this one. One never knows how a story will travel over time and place - and for the unfolding of this book, I give thanks to all who contributed to its journey. A special acknowledgement goes to Jud Cure, who never gave up on bringing this story to print, and to Jean Tarbox for her exacting wordcraft, aligning text to images. Finally, I thank Raven, for calling all of us together inside this book.

As Raven flew high above the forest canopy, the sun was just beginning to wane, casting a golden orange blaze across the clear, daylight sky. As far as the eye could see, the evergreen forest lay ahead and below her. Soon the cool wind from the coast would carry her further towards the sea. She anticipated the coastline grasses waving and greeting her as she flew overhead.

Raven chose a landing spot on the upper branch of a silver needle pine. She cocked her head, listening, first to one side and then the other; then pulled her head forward to fluff her throat feathers and greet her companions in the wild. With a clear, loud tone, she let out first one call, and then another, *Korr! Korr!* Her call lingered in the air, reverberating like a question.

Raven waited for the familiar echo of her voice to bounce off the white pines ahead. As she waited for a sound to touch the feathers around her prominent beak, a wave of fear rippled through her body. She tried again, *Korr! Korr!*

The silence was unexpected and eerie. Something was wrong. With her feathers bristling down her back, Raven prepared to investigate. Thrusting her head upward, she was lifted higher by Wind as she glided gently into flight.

Further ahead, the forest tree line dropped into a cavernous gash below. As Raven came closer, a devastating sight met her gaze. What her eyes saw, her body already knew.

There, where an elegant community of spruce trees had been, with their long silvery needles stirring in the Wind, was now a ruin of dying tree stumps. Exposed to the full force of the sun, the biome of the tree's understory would soon be destroyed.

Seeing it like that was so overwhelming she became disoriented and faltered. The weight of her loss pulled her down, and the rhythmic cadence of her wings going forward failed her. It was as if she, too, were being plundered.

Raven landed on a stump of freshly cut pine. The air was full of its scent. Its inner bark, exposed unnaturally to the light, gave off an acrid, pungent odor.

A trickle of sap still seeped down its sides. Raven's nose and eyes stung. A nasty smell remained in the air. Gasoline.

Raven's beautiful forest and creatures she loved were all gone. As her beak opened, a single, warbling cry of despair croaked out its lament.

Large silver tears formed and fell from her eyes, unleashing a torrent of grief. Water misted the world and swallowed Raven's sight – a world that had suddenly been turned upside down.

In her grief, Raven turned from her suffering to the lament of absence. All that nothingness. Everything she loved the most, destroyed. The tall trees, the forest, her friends, all emptied. All that made her loss so much harder to bear.

In her sorrow, her mind turned to the last time she had visited the forest. How she loved to play tricks on the others! She knew how to find just the right stick with which to bat pinecones and small stones. She swatted them with a stick held tightly in her beak. She even enticed Wolf to play, nudging a stone with his paw back and forth. What a delight when another creature would play, too! What fun they had together!

Best trick of all was how she could use non-vocal gestures to trick others into thinking she was a mammal instead of a bird!! Even more laughable, Raven loved to imitate Wolf's call so she could scare Fox away. Happiness was pranking Jay with a decoy, pretending to hide her food in one place, only to taunt and mock him falling for it being there. Oh, she was very good at impersonation!

II

Now, all their playful exchanges would never happen again. Those words, 'never again', echoed and disappeared into the darkness of Raven's despair. The silence of all that nothingness was deafening. A deep pain pierced her heart. How could she ever survive it?

Alone and lonely, a whirlwind of emotions struck her like a lightning bolt. An inner explosion followed that shattered her into a million pieces of grief. Raven's heart was broken.

A deep shadow pulled at her feathers, leaving a terrible chill. "All the things I will never know again!" she lamented.

The anger that arose afterwards was immediate and certain. The trees plundered. Gone with the trees, the life of the forest was also emptied. With the trees, the lives of its creatures had also been clearcut. Without the protection of its canopy, soon even the forest soil would become unable to bear the life of another tree.

"Why?" she cried out. Korr? Korr? Korr? "Why, why, why?" Her beak as wide open as a baby bird's waiting for food, she called out a long, broken cry of grief. It returned no morsel. Inconsolable, she hopped into the understory at the base of the stump and burrowed her head into her feathers. Under the canopy of the night sky, she cried herself to sleep.

As Raven slept, she dreamt that she was falling, journeying through the tree stump into the center of the earth. She fell so deeply that she entered the stump's roots, and became one with its nutrients.

She moved swiftly into the root's meandering ectoplasm, rushing through its arteries. With its twisting intersections, she traveled through the capillaries and was carried inside a meandering torrent of shapeshifting plasma.

Suddenly, she stopped her descent. As she landed on a soft earthen cloud, the darkness embraced her. Nothingness enveloped her in a warm caress, soothing her immense longing for a once familiar world.

Within the comfort of this inner sanctuary, Raven surrendered to the darkness without danger or fear. Slowly, her grief released its grip and she rested, within the softness of a peaceful calm.

Ever so faintly, Raven began to hear an *almost* sound. The *almost* sound was so far away and diminished, it was *almost* not there. Quietly and slowly, it grew into a single note - a sound so melodious and full of love, it was *almost* all encompassing. It brought comfort to every cell of her being. As it grew more intense, the tone became so loud she started vibrating. The vibration shook her to the very core.

Inside herself she saw an *almost* light. The tiny pinprick in the darkness grew bigger and brighter until Raven was completely covered by its illumination. It grew and grew until the light reached everywhere and became everything. The light broke into colors that began to change and shape shift with remarkable beauty. The intensity of the Light matched the intensity of the sound. As they reached a common pitch, both light and sound began to dance together.

The colors danced into each other, becoming a moving tapestry of sound and light, gently touching Raven's body. The living benevolence kissed Raven's tears with recognition and quieted them.

Raven felt an embrace that touched her broken heart. With loving support, she crossed the threshold of brokenness and remembered when she entered the forest for the first time. Being unconditionally loved was both innocent and curious. Now, as she surrendered to the feeling of pure love, it was like a blessing of grace. And then the Light spoke.

"Raven, thank you for your kind heart and loving compassion. We recognize you, beloved. Your tears are felt by us, too. Today we came to show you something important."

The words penetrated her being as the shifting, golden presence continued. "There is something from deep within you that the world needs, Raven."

At once, the glorious Light wrapped itself wholly around her and carried her like a cloud, up and out of her sanctuary to the place where the grasslands met the sea - the ecotone of the forest. From her cloud haven, Raven noticed the area swarming with life. Many kinds of ecosystem friends scuttled back and forth between the grass, sand, and sea, carrying debris and food back to their homes. Raven saw many marvelous things happening at once.

Raven watched Dragonfly hovering over a freshwater pool near the sea. Her translucent wings, streaked with colors, sent bright iridescent flashes of light swirling and dancing together.

This light play attracted young fish who were drawn to bask in its shimmering iridescence before scurrying away. Raven watched how the light bounced from its wings to the water and back again, forming a rainbow bridge at the surface. Dragonfly brought a beautiful dance of light into the world with her presence.

A dead insect on its back was being carried unsteadily by many tiny creatures helping one another. Nearby, Red Ant was chewing up pieces of rotting bark and carrying it into camouflaged tunnels. The masticated material passed from one ant to another in an unstoppable flow. Red Ant was busy bringing food not only to serve its Queen, but to benefit many other organisms. In a life-saving supply of nutrients, these decomposers also brought in fungi and bacteria to help aerate the soil, helping all creatures. The soil in turn supported the growth of the tall trees – the lungs of the earth - in symbiosis with the web of life.

Near the water, Raven noticed how Songbird's melodic trills were carried up into the air like moving musical notes. Each sound left thin, nearly imperceptible patterns in the sky. The patterns moved with the rhythmic flow of the air until they eventually dissolved, impossible to see.

Songbird's tones touched one bird at a time until all the birds of the forest woke up and sang together, joining one another in a symphony of melodious trilling. Again, the Light spoke, "The sounds that surround you are part of your own *heart*song, Raven. Every living thing has one. All the world is alive and responds to your presence with its own wisdom. That's the hope you bring to the world – that it is possible to cooperate with all of *life* itself.

"Take a look around this beauty, Raven. This is the forest of your heart. Notice how it responds to the love you bring it." What unfolded next in front of Raven was a vision of the forest fully regenerated – healthy, safe, and restored. She witnessed the forest, with all its mystery, cooperating with the lifeforce around it as one, unified ecosystem. This interactive field of creation was pulsing with life. Sun fed the splendor with a brilliance so strong that Light itself fractured and sent rainbow fractals everywhere. All around Raven, her *heart*song vibrated.

Light explained, "When you offer an invitation to life to cooperate with what you need, you become part of a great cycle of dynamic change. Each morning is a new day, Raven. Each one makes it so with their own *heart*song. Look for the invisible good inside everything you see."

When Raven returned from her dream, the world was beginning to awaken. The golden presence was gone. She looked around the desecrated forest with new eyes. As she watched, tiny creatures of all sizes and colors moved about, creeping, crawling, flying, walking, hopping, or sliding. They were all busy making use of what was left. Cricket's melodious song caught her attention. Serrations on the edges of Cricket's wings as they rose to rub together created a repetitive sound that chirped all around her.

"Why are you singing so loudly, Cricket?" Raven asked. "I am singing for the pleasure of singing," exclaimed Cricket. "I express how much I love the world."

"I wish I knew how to sing like that," Raven answered. Suddenly, she heard another voice calling out to her. Like the dream, an orange Dragonfly appeared nearby. Its iridescent wings glittered in the sun, catching its light and magnifying it around her.

"Dragonfly, what are you doing this morning?" asked Raven.

"I'm planting seeds of hope," she replied, dropping something from her razer sharp teeth and legs. "Just like you."

"Like me?" exclaimed Raven. "How?" "You will see," Dragonfly answered, before darting away to its mission, its *heart*tsong sending a shimmer of rainbows sparkling in the air, lighting up the world.

"Now it's your turn, Raven. What do *you* sing for?" Cricket asked. Raven remembered how one single tone in her dream had touched her feelings and enveloped her in total peace. She responded, "I will sing for my helpers to come restore the Forest." And with that, Raven pulled up her head and ruffled her feathers. With the full force of her breath, she touched the feeling of the tone and breathed it out.

Raven pushed that tone around and played with it, testing it and turning it over. The tone took form and flew out into the world, almost on its own. Tones summersaulted from high pitched delight to low, guttural warbles of affection. It was all Raven's own *heart*song, glued together by one common tone of love.

Suddenly, Raven knew how simple it was. "Thank you, Dragonfly!" Raven let her *heart*song announce itself to the plundered forest and then took flight following Dragonfly over to the grasslands by the sea.

Raven's large build and wingspan moved in the sky like a giant shadow. She landed on a low hanging tree by the edge of the sea and called out to the creatures close and far.

Her song traveled farther than the eye could see and reverberated like an echo, rippling across the sky to the sea. Just as the Light had instructed her, she sang her *heart*song as an invitation for creation to help her. Wind helped her fly easily to the edge of the freshwater tributary.

There, a great orchestration of collective effort was underway. Light shimmered in the meadow of the tall grasslands, becoming an oasis for many species of birds, animals and insects. Birds from all tribes fluttered about, cooing, and splashing and pecking - leaving patterns of tiny holes in the sandy soil.

Raven watched as Butterfly planted a spherical egg on the underside of a leaf, making it immobile. Secured in its place, the color of the egg told her it would produce a caterpillar too toxic to eat.

"Butterfly", Raven called, "how do you know if your egg will live long enough to pupate?" "I don't," Butterfly replied. "But I still follow the signs of nature to lay my eggs in protected places. It's a cycle that has occurred for millions of years."

And with that, Butterfly began to sing to its intended future butterfly. The song was sweet and joyous. Its sounds fluttered, mirroring the way Butterfly danced above the egg with delight.

Into this oasis, a new mystery was unfolding. And suddenly Raven had an idea. She flew closer to the sea and rested on a rock. Raven's *heart*song called out to Water creatures near and far to come close.

Her tones rose and fell like birds, modulating from one pitch into another, until vibrating together. Her *heart*song traveled across the sea, sky, and land as an invitation for all creation to come help regenerate the forest. Wind came and carried Raven's tones to where she intended them to reach.

As if hearing the soothing heartbeat of a mother, aquatic creatures slowly came to life. And so they swam closer, answering her call. "Sea dragons, prepare yourselves to bring the rain," Raven's *heart*song commanded. And so they came from afar, coming from sea, sky, and land.

In a long, echoing *heart*song, Raven called next to the creatures of the Air.

Moving slowly through the clouds came a clan of many hues, sizes and shapes - the Sky Dragons. Some were golden orange; others shimmered opalescent or were tinged with maroon. Watching their arrival, Raven tingled with delight.

Sky Dragons welcomed her as they slowly surrounded her in their soft, luxurious sweetness. Tears of belonging brimmed in her eyes. "Sky dragons, help us locate the best places to plant new seeds in the clear-cut forest," Raven's *heart*song asked, and they continued on their quest.

Soon Raven was answered by Sky's companions in the Wind - flying creatures of all kinds from all species, habitats, and directions.

Came Crow, Songbird, the Common Yellowthroat, Eagle and Hawk. Later came Duck and Loon. "Follow us!" Raven sang as she took flight with all the clans further inland. As the creatures flew together, Raven pushed her head up to feel Wind touching the feathers around her neck. Together with relatives from the marine coast and forest, the Bird Tribes took Raven's instructions to peck holes in the ground around the clear-cut tree stumps.

As they passed over the freshwater tributary, Raven called out to Dragonfly. "Dragonfly," Raven's *heart*song called, "with your razer-sharp teeth, please carry seeds from foraged pinecones into the clear-cut forest and drop them inside Bird's new holes in the ground." In reply, Dragonfly hovered nearby, and then darted straight away to the freshwater tributary, inviting her brothers and sisters to come help, too.

Next, Raven went to look for Ant. Debris from tunnels dug in the earthen ground marked Ant's territory. Just as in her dream, Raven observed the active creatures passing back and forth between one destination and another. Moving together like a living plasma, the ants worked together as life-saving ecosystem engineers, carrying nutrients and oxygen to the soil. "Ant!" Raven called.

"Raven, we don't have ears! We feel the vibrations of your sounds through our feet. Just as we feel the meaning of your words without hearing them." Raven's toning shook the ground so Ant would know the meaning of her vibrations. Next, Raven bent her head close to the ground to listen to their response. "We can help you, Raven! Tell us how you want us to assist." In reply Raven stomped, "Tunnel under the new seeds and carry bits of compost there so they have the right conditions for growth!"

Raven watched the critters scurry away, covering themselves with shelter. Everyone except Ant, who was already protected in tunnels underground. Taking shelter herself, Raven stopped to contemplate what they had all done together.

They had faced the catastrophe of destruction and planted seeds of hope for the future. It wasn't just a dream. Her *heart*song had brought the help she needed. As they continued to cooperate, they would find ways to work together to protect the tiny seedlings until the new trees could mature and become an intact forest again. The forest and its families could regenerate anew. Raven nestled in the dry understory of her new home, content in the knowledge her home would be regenerated.

It was just the beginning. All cooperators would slowly but surely bring the forest back to life. Her dream showed her the importance of contributing something that only she could give. Her *heart*song had been answered by others to accomplish the vision of restoration. Raven recognized that each *heart*song was needed to support the health and well-being of the forest ecosystem.

Her inner knowing had revealed how visions of hope can activate the forces of life itself. Raven knew one day she would wake again into a newly restored community of the living forest. Happy in this renewal, Raven drifted into sleep once more.

About Raven

Raven is one of Nature's most interesting creatures. Besides primates, Raven is the only other creature who make toys to play with. With its beak to pick up sticks, Raven uses sticks as a tool to push, pull, take, hit, and pass rocks and pinecones to other birds and animals, especially wolves, otters and dogs. Because Raven can adapt to any habitat, there are several species of Raven around the world. Some Ravens in winter climates use their outstretched wings to slide down thick slopes of snow on rooftops, as if they were a toboggan. Ever the optimist for play, Raven likes to imitate the calls of other birds and animals, too, and uses them to steer predators away from its nest and food. Considered a great trickster in many cultures, Raven lives as an enduring symbol and subject of many myths, stories and legends around the world.

About This Book

Raven flies into her favorite woods and finds her forest playground is gone. In her grief, she follows the guidance of a dream and goes on a journey to find regeneration for her heart and ultimately for the forest, her home.

In her quest, Raven discovers that she has a unique song to sing that comes from her heart. Using her *heart*song, she calls out to sea, sky, and land creatures for help to restore her beloved forest. By gathering together in common purpose, they seed the clear-cut ground for new life to emerge.

Raven reminds us it is possible to connect to the living wisdom of all creatures and the Earth and to steward the health of damaged ecosystems and nurture them back to life.

For the Reader

In this story, Raven discovers how to find a song of love and hope out of the destruction and loss. Her determination to call others to help her restore the forest ecosystem, leads her on an inner journey through a dream. There she finds the greatest light of all radiating out through her heart, emanating her love for the forest and all it nurtures.

Her powerful love and its magnificence, gives her the courage to act. With determination, she is able to find and sing her unique *heart*song, giving her hope for renewal. As Raven communicates with the world, the world does too, with her. Other forest creatures and ecosystem engineers reciprocate, joining with her quest and becoming a part of a living community – all working together in a common purpose to preserve and sustain the health of the forest.

Reflection

How do you interpret the meaning of Raven's *Heart*song as a story and a metaphor? How does it affect you and what message do you hear from Raven's call? Can Raven's quest serve as a guidepost for the inner journey of contemplation? What are your beacons of light leading the way forward with life's challenges? Like Raven, play with your tonal signature as sound. Discover the joy of releasing your own sound through the act of singing wordless tones and how they affect you.

Investigate the note that announces your presence in the world and is yours alone. Explore what it means to you. Raven's journey encourages each person to find their own unique song and to bring forth the music of their heart. Contemplate how touching your own soul song benefits you and those around you as a gift bestowed.

What is Your HeartSong?

Each person brings their own unique *heart*song into the world. Like handwriting, *heart*song is one's own, unique signature. No one can give you a *heart*song and no one can take it away. It is always only yours.

A *heart*song begins with making a wordless tone and sounding it out. A sound can be created from one tone or several notes put together in their own unique way. A tone can be its own song or modulate from a continuous sound.

Because sound touches everything in its path, sounds contribute its vibration to every living thing directly or by proximity. And this is how a *heart*song travels out into the world touching others.

HeartSong Practice

How do you find the right sound that represents only you? A good place to start is releasing a sound, any sound. Let your breath release and carry any sound your voice wants to make. Like a caress or a hug, releasing wordless sounds is something you can do each day.

To find your own *heart*song, play around with how tones feel. Amplify their effects. Throw the tones around like Raven would, wondering about and finding out what they do. Let your voice play with itself like Raven does.

Let go of what restrains you. Study what it's for and how it works best for you. With practice, you will know.

About the Author

Teresa M. Tipton has brought the arts to life for learners of all ages Internationally as an artist, writer, teacher, and coach. Her characters are drawn from diverse cultural experience working in the USA, Tanzania, China, Czech Republic, Kenya, and Taiwan  and collaborations in Japan, Portugal, Brazil, and Spain. This book first began in a remote part of the Amazon forest, when she came upon clear-cut groves, further destroyed by fire and cattle, imperiling the Amazon's future and motivating this story.

Carrying on a distinguished history of service in her family, she enjoys creating arts and education opportunities for children of all ages and collaborating with other artists and organizations. She is devoted to developing new ways of knowing through the arts and is committed to bringing the future into whole child education today. By her words and art, she hopes to inspire each person to action in ways that protect and sustain the well-being of the earth's many ecosystems for the next generations to come.

Printed in the United States
by Baker & Taylor Publisher Services